GIRLZ

Pool Rats

Holly Smith Dinbergs

illustrated by
Monika Maddock

MACMILLAN

First published in 2005 by
MACMILLAN EDUCATION AUSTRALIA PTY LTD
627 Chapel Street, South Yarra 3141

Visit our website at www.macmillan.com.au

Associated companies and representatives throughout the world.

National Library of Australia
Cataloguing-in-Publication data

Smith Dinbergs, Holly.

  Pool pals.

  For primary school students.
  ISBN 0 7329 9880 8.
  ISBN 0 7329 9876 X (series).

  1. Swimming – Juvenile fiction. I. Title. (Series:
  Girlz rock!).

A823.4

Series created by Felice Arena and Phil Kettle
Project Management by Limelight Press Pty Ltd
Cover and text design by Lore Foye
Illustrations by Monika Maddock

Printed in Australia by McPherson's Printing Group

GIRLZROCK!
Contents

Jules   *Rosa*

CHAPTER 1

Early Morning Meet

Jules is upstairs in her bedroom
when her best friend Rosa arrives.
A few seconds later, Rosa throws her
backpack on the bed and flops down
beside the bag.

Jules "You didn't take long to settle
in. Sure you're comfortable there?"

Rosa laughs, then settles back onto the pillow on the bed.

Rosa "You ready for the school swimming carnival?"

Jules "Guess so. I can't believe it's come around again so quickly."

Rosa "Me neither—I'll be happy when it's all over."

Jules "I wish you could've slept over here last night."

Rosa "I know, but Dad was afraid we'd talk all night. He said I needed to get a good night's sleep before the carnival."

Jules "Remember the last time you stayed over? We didn't go to sleep until almost four in the morning. Mum wasn't happy."

Rosa "Only because of that shadow
we saw outside the window."

Jules "The one that turned out to
be a harmless possum?"

Rosa "Yeah, sucked right in! Let's see
if I can sleep over this weekend."

Jules "Okay, and we can plan a midnight raid on the kitchen."

Rosa "Great. I'm putting chocolate biscuits on the search list!"

Jules's mother yells upstairs that it's time to leave.

Jules "Well, this is it."

Rosa "I'm totally nervous, aren't you? But you don't need to be— you're such a good swimmer. You won nearly every race last year."

Jules "Yeah, but I had my lucky anklet then."

Rosa "How could I forget! You never stop talking about it."

Jules "Well, it was special and I can't believe I lost it."

Rosa "I know, but that won't stop you swimming well. Just remember what Mr. Zammit says."

Jules "As if I ever could. He really drums that chant into us like some war cry or something."

Jules and Rosa "You can do it, I can do it, we all can do it!"

The girls chant all way down the stairs. They race outside to the car where Jules's mother is waiting.

Rosa "Oh, wait! I've left my bag in your room."

8

Rosa runs back inside. After a few minutes, she still hasn't returned.

Jules (calling out) "Rosa, where are you? We do want to make the first race, y'know."

A moment later Rosa's back in the car and they all head off to the pool.

CHAPTER 2

Butterfly Babes

Jules says goodbye to her mum.
Then the girls head inside with all
the other kids.

Jules "Race ya to the changing rooms!"

Rosa "You know we're not s'posed to run."

Jules "Then let's power walk. The teachers can't get us for that. It's good exercise."

As the girls take off, Jules puts her
towel around her shoulders like a
cape. Rosa is right behind her.

Rosa "Jules, you look like a
   butterfly—with really long legs."
Jules "What d'you mean?"
Rosa "When you walk fast like that,
   the air puffs your towel out like
   butterfly wings."

Jules "Oh, cool, I love butterflies."

Rosa decides to do the same with her towel.

Rosa "Look at us. We're butterfly babes."

Jules "Yeah, or pool pals."

Once in the change rooms, the
girls get into their bathers, then walk
out to the pool.

Rosa "Wow! Look how crowded this
place is."

Jules "The teachers'll call us over soon to start racing. Wanna get wet first?"

Rosa "Okay, let's go together. One, two, three ..."

CHAPTER 3

Go Rosa!

After warming up in the water, all the kids hop out of the pool, ready to begin the carnival.

Rosa "It's almost time for my race."

Jules "You're gonna be great."

Rosa "Hope so, but I'm really nervous."

Rosa lines up for her event—the 100-metre freestyle.

Jules "Good luck, Rosa!"

Rosa "I just don't want to come last."

Jules "You won't. Hey look, there's your dad."

Rosa looks up to see her dad and mum in the crowd. They smile and wave at the girls. Rosa walks towards the starting blocks.

Rosa (talking to herself) "I can do it. I can do it."

Rosa and the other swimmers line up at the end of the pool. The starter raises his pistol then *bang!* and Rosa dives in.

Jules "Go, Rosa, go! Go, Rosa, go!"

As Rosa approaches the end of the first lap, Jules screams even louder.

Jules "Rosa, get ready to turn, now turn. One lap to go!"

Rosa touches the wall and turns. She's just behind the fastest swimmer. With less than a metre to go, she reaches for the finishing wall. Jules runs up to her.

Jules "That was amazing!"

Rosa "But I didn't win."

Jules "Yeah, but ya came second. That's totally cool. I hope I can do that well, even without my lucky anklet."

Rosa "You will. You gotta forget about that anklet and just go for it."

CHAPTER 4

Jules's Big Moment

An announcement echoes around the pool that the next event is about to begin.

Rosa "Now, it's your race, Jules. Good luck!"

Jules moves to the edge of the pool in lane 3. She notices Rosa smiling with her towel around her shoulders like butterfly wings. *Bang!* and Jules dives in.

Rosa (cheering) "Go, Jules, go!"

Jules speeds up the pool and takes
the lead. There's a girl in green
bathers in the next lane. By the
second lap, the girl has moved slightly
ahead of her. Jules tries to swim faster.

Rosa "C'mon Jules, you're almost
    winning. I can do it! You can do it!
    We all ..."

With every stroke, Jules gains on the girl in the green bathers.

Jules (thinking as she swims along) "She looks like a crocodile. I can beat an old croc!"

Jules is spurred on even more. Suddenly she slaps the wall of the pool with her hand. She looks up to see Rosa.

Rosa "You won! You won!"

Jules gets out of the pool and the girls jump up and down excitedly, hugging each other.

Jules "This is so cool. I thought that crocodile was going to beat me."

Rosa "Crocodile?"

Jules "Forget it, my eyes were playing tricks on me out there. I can't believe I won that race."

CHAPTER 5

Surprise! Surprise!

After the carnival, the girls go back
to Jules's house. They are tired, but
are both really happy about Jules's
win. They race straight upstairs to
Jules's bedroom.

Jules "What's this sign on my door? 'Congratulations'—who did this? And a present. This is so weird. My birthday's not till next week."

Rosa starts to laugh.

Rosa "I did it. I only pretended to
leave my bag in your room this
morning so I had an excuse to come
back and hang up the sign. I made
it for you last night because ... well,
I just knew that you'd win today."

Jules "But I really thought I'd lose
without my lucky anklet."

Rosa "Well, there you go, you didn't,
you won all by yourself."

Jules smiles and rips the ribbon
and wrapping paper off the present.

Jules "Oh, mad! Another anklet. It's
so cool, better than the one I lost. I
just love it … thanks Ro."

Rosa "It's an early birthday present,
a new lucky anklet. But I don't
think you need it anymore. You
rocked today!"

Jules "So did you. This anklet is so beautiful. I wish I had something for you."

Rosa "Um ... well, maybe you have."

Jules "Really? What?"

Rosa "How about some chocolate biscuits?"

Jules

GIRLZ ROCK!
Swimming Lingo

Rosa

butterfly An insect, and also a swimming stroke that requires strong shoulders and stomach muscles.

lane The area of the pool marked off by special ropes where you swim if you compete in a race.

lane lines The dividers used to mark the lanes for a swimming race. They are often special ropes designed to keep the water calm during a race.

lap One length of a pool.

tumble turn When you turn around at the end of the pool after a lap. You do a forward somersault through the water so you end up facing the opposite end of the pool.

GIRLZ ROCK!

Swimming Must-dos

☆ Don't just wear a swimsuit when you swim. Put sunscreen on too.

☆ Don't forget to bring a towel.

☆ Ask your parents for a pair of goggles if you don't like water in your eyes.

☆ Don't breathe underwater. Get a pair of nose plugs if you don't like water in your nose.

☆ If you get a lot of ear infections, wear earplugs in the water.

☆ If you don't want to get your hair wet, wear a cool swimming cap.

☆ Learn to do a tumble turn, especially if you want to set a world record. It's way faster and you look way cool!

☆ Always swim with a friend. It's more fun and if one of you has a problem, the other one can get help.

GIRLZ ROCK!

Swimming Instant Info

An Olympic sized pool is 50 metres long and 25 metres wide.

The Olympic Games, which started in 776 BC for men only, included women's swimming events for the first time in 1912.

Today, there are 16 swimming races in the Olympic Games.

Dawn Fraser, Shane Gould and Susie O'Neill are all famous Australian swimming legends.

Elephants can swim up to 32 kilometres a day. They use their trunk as a natural snorkel.

Hungarian, Krisztina Egerszegi, holds the world record for winning the most gold medals in women's swimming at the Olympics. She has won gold medals for the 100-metre backstroke (1992), the 200-metre backstroke (1988, 1992, 1996) and the 400-metre medley (1992).

 There are four main swimming strokes: backstroke, breaststroke, butterfly and freestyle (which some people call the Australian crawl).

 Kangaroos are excellent swimmers.

 The temperature in the pool at the Olympics is usually between 25°C and 28°C.

GIRLZ ROCK!

Think Tank

1 If a tortoise and a dolphin swam in a race, who do you think would win?

2 Can a butterfly actually swim?

3 How long is an Olympic-sized pool?

4 What Australian animal is a really good swimmer?

5 Which swimming stroke has the same name as an insect?

6 How many swimming events are in the Olympic Games?

7 Where do swimmers hang out?

8 What's the best way to turn around when you swim in a pool?

Answers

1 The dolphin would beat the tortoise because it is a much faster creature.

2 No—a butterfly cannot actually swim.

3 An Olympic-sized pool is 50 metres long.

4 A kangaroo is a really good swimmer.

5 The butterfly stroke has the same name as an insect.

6 There are 16 swimming events in the Olympic Games.

7 Swimmers hang out by the pool, of course!

8 The best way to turn around in a pool is to do a tumble turn.

How did you score?

- If you got all 8 answers correct, then you're ready to start training for the Olympics. So get your goggles on!

- If you got 6 answers correct, then maybe you can be a lifeguard at the pool (get your safety certificate first!).

- If you got fewer than 4 answers correct, you might want to take a few more swimming lessons or watch from the side of the pool.

Hey Girls!

I love to read and hope you do, too. The first book I really loved was called "Mary Poppins". It was full of magic (way before Harry Potter) and it got me hooked on reading. I went to the library every Saturday and left with a pile of books so heavy I could hardly carry them!

Here are some ideas about how you can make "Pool Pals" even more fun. At school, you and your friends can be actors and put on this story as a play. To bring the story to life, bring in some props from home such as a big towel and an ankle bracelet. Maybe you can set up an area in the room to look like starting blocks for a pool race.

Who will be Jules? Who will be Rosa? Who will be the narrator? (That's the person who reads the parts between when Jules or Rosa say something.) Once you know who's going to do what, you're ready to act out the story in front of the class. I bet everyone will clap when you are finished. Hey, a talent scout from a television station may be watching!

See if somebody at home will read this story out loud with you. Reading at home is important and a lot of fun as well.

You know what my dad used to tell me? Readers are leaders!

And, remember, Girlz Rock!

GIRLZ ROCK!
When We Were Kids

Holly

Julie

Holly talked with Julie, another *Girlz Rock!* author

Holly "Were you a good swimmer when you were a kid?"

Julie "Yeah, I loved it! I was really good at butterfly."

Holly "I used to go to the pool with my girlfriends and look at the cute lifeguards."

Julie "Were you a good swimmer?"

Holly "Well, I was a better diver. I could do a back flip. But if you don't quite finish a back flip, it's a belly flop."

Julie "Ouch. I'll stick to butterfly."

Holly "Yeah, a butterfly would beat a belly flop any day!"

GIRLZROCK!
What a Laugh!

Q Why did the swimming star throw her toast out the window?

A She wanted to see butter fly.

GIRLZROCK!

Read about the fun
that girls have in these
GIRLZROCK! titles:

Hair Scare

Diary Disaster

Netball Showdown

The Sleepover

Bowling Buddies

School Play Stars

Pool Pals

Horsing Around

Girl Pirates

Surf Girls